The people of Etheria love their Princess Adora, who is gentle and good. But there are times when Princess Adora becomes She-Ra, Princess of Power, riding Swift Wind, her winged unicorn. Those are the times when she has magic powers to defend the country against the forces of evil, or simply to help someone in trouble.

British Library Cataloguing in Publication Data

Grant, John
    She-Ra and the surprise party. — (She-Ra Princess of Power; v. 5)
    I. Title   II. Gabbey, Terry   III. Series
    823'.914[J]   PZ7
    ISBN 0-7214-0981-4

First edition

Published by Ladybird Books Ltd Loughborough Leicestershire UK
Ladybird Books Inc Lewiston Maine 04240 USA

She-Ra and the surprise party

by John Grant
illustrated by Terry Gabbey

Ladybird Books

One afternoon, Princess Adora was riding through
Whispering Wood. In a clearing stood a crowd of
Twiggets. "Good morning," called Adora. "It's a
lovely day."

"Shh!" said the Twiggets, fingers to lips. One of
them pointed upwards into the branches of a tree.
"It's Kowl," he said. "He's busy. Counting."

Adora looked up through the leaves at the portly
figure of Kowl. He was frowning, and muttering to
himself as he counted on his fingers. He saw Adora
looking up, and stopped.

"You're right," he said to the Twiggets. "It's in a week's time."

"What is?" asked Adora.

"Madame Razz's birthday," said Kowl.

"And what are you planning to do about it?" asked Adora.

"Do about it?" said the Twiggets. "Wish her many happy returns, most likely."

"Give her a present," said Kowl.

"What about a birthday party?" asked Adora.

Adora told her friend Glimmer about her idea of a birthday party for Madame Razz. "What a good idea," said Glimmer. "But let's make it a surprise for her."

Glimmer went home to tell her mother, Queen Angella, about it. The Queen said, "Wonderful! It is many years since the Great Hall of Castle Brightmoon was used for anything special. We will have the party there. The Royal Cooks can start right away on the preparations. And the Royal Musicians have a whole week to practise playing their brightest dance tunes."

As the Queen had said, Castle Brightmoon was soon bustling with activity. Tables, chairs, cups, plates, knives and forks were brought out from the Castle store rooms.

And, during all the preparations, not a word was said to Madame Razz.

It was, after all, to be a complete surprise.

Adora, Glimmer and Kowl sat down to make out a guest list.

"I know it's a funny thing to say," exclaimed Kowl, "but things would be a lot easier if Madame Razz hadn't so many friends."

He checked the list for the hundredth time. "Oh, dear! We've forgotten Prince Defiant."

"Do you think Frosta, the Ice Empress, will come?" said Adora.

"It's too warm for her in Etheria," said Glimmer. "But I know she would like to be asked just the same."

"Well, that seems to be that," said Kowl, running his finger down the list for the last time.

"I think we should ask Catra," said Adora.

"CATRA!" cried Kowl and Glimmer together. "After all the trouble she's caused us?"

"I know," said Adora, "but I still think we should be nice to her when we can. She's not *completely* bad. If we are kind to her, perhaps some day she may mend her ways."

"You may be right," said Kowl, reluctantly. And he added Catra's name to the list.

The invitations were sent out...in secret. It was not easy. Madame Razz seemed to be everywhere at once.

One of the braver Twiggets took Catra's invitation. Trembling, he made his way through the Fright Zone to the Cat Tower. Then he crept fearfully to the door, slipped the invitation under it, and ran as fast as his legs would carry him.

Catra read the invitation. "So there is to be a surprise party for Madame Razz," she said to Clawdeen. "And *I* have been invited. There must be a catch somewhere. How would they like it if I were to tell Madame Razz of the party? That would spoil the surprise...and repay Adora and the rest for all the times they have interfered in my affairs."

"I have a better idea," purred Clawdeen. "Accept the invitation. Send a present — I'll tell you what to send. If all goes according to plan, the party will be — er — interrupted, and Madame Razz's birthday gifts will be in more deserving hands. Ours!"

In the week before the party, all manner of parcels and packages arrived at Castle Brightmoon. These were birthday presents for Madame Razz. Queen Angella and Glimmer and the Castle servants were kept busy setting them out in the Great Hall.

With one last day to go, a letter and a large box were delivered to the Castle. They were from Catra. The letter was to accept the invitation, and the box contained Catra's birthday present to Madame Razz.

Queen Angella looked at the box thoughtfully. "I think we'd better just look at this present," she said.

It was a cat. Not a real cat, but one made out of a strange green metal. There were joints in the metal. It was some sort of mechanical toy.

"It frightens me," said Glimmer, looking at it. "I know that it isn't real, but it has a wicked look. It's the eyes, I think."

The eyes of the metal cat were black. Not shiny black, but dull and lifeless. There was nothing to say what the cat did, or how to set it in motion. Catra would no doubt explain all that when she came to the party.

On the night before the party, Adora sat down
with her friends to check that nothing had been
forgotten. Piles of presents were stacked high all
around the hall. They came from all Madame Razz's
friends... but there was nothing from the Twiggets!
"The Twiggets are preparing a surprise present," said
Glimmer. "I don't know what it is to be, but they
spend a lot of time giggling among themselves!"

"Whatever else happens," said Queen Angella, "Madame Razz must know nothing until the very last moment."

"But," said Glimmer, "she is bound to notice everyone is dressed in their best clothes, and heading for Castle Brightmoon. Someone will have to keep her busy until we are ready to spring the surprise."

"Leave that to me," said Adora.

Early next morning, Adora saddled her horse Spirit and rode through Whispering Wood in search of Madame Razz. She found her in a clearing practising her magic. And it wasn't going well at all. She waved her arms. She muttered magic words. And Broom leaned against a tree looking worried. When Madame Razz's magic went wrong, Broom was usually the one who suffered.

Adora called out, "Good morning, Madame Razz!"

Madame Razz stopped her waving and muttering.
She sat down on a tree stump to get her breath
back, and Adora joined her.

"It's one of *those* mornings," said Madame Razz.
"It's really a very simple piece of magic. But it just
won't come right. You see that toadstool? I should
be able to magic it right to the other side of the
clearing. And back again. Or anywhere else. And it
doesn't work."

"Can I help in any way?" asked Adora.

"The only person who can help me is my old
teacher, Madame Whizz. But she lives far away
among the Sylvan Mountains."

Adora slipped away, leaving Madame Razz to her practice. She mounted Spirit and rode off into the trees. Once she was out of sight she drew her sword and cried:

"FOR THE HONOUR OF GRAYSKULL!"

In an instant she had become She-Ra, Princess of Power, and Spirit was Swift Wind, the fabulous winged unicorn.

Madame Razz was still trying hard when she looked up and saw Swift Wind swooping down over the tree tops. He landed beside her.

"It's such a lovely day," said She-Ra, "that I would like to give Swift Wind some exercise. Perhaps a flight to the Sylvan Mountains for the day."

"Did you say the Sylvan Mountains!" exclaimed Madame Razz. "Do you think that I could...that is to say, would you...?"

"Would you like to come?" asked She-Ra.

"Yes, please!" cried Madame Razz.

In no time at all, Swift Wind was soaring high above Whispering Wood. Madame Razz clung behind She-Ra, with Broom tucked firmly under her arm.

"I like this!" cried Broom. "Carrying people around is part of the job of being a magic broom, but it's nice being carried for a change."

Soon the Sylvan Mountains appeared ahead. "Is there any place in particular you would like to visit?" asked She-Ra.

Madame Razz looked down. "Yes," she said. "I have a friend who lives here. Her house has a pink roof and green chimney. The walls are brown with yellow decorations."

Swift Wind swooped lower.

"There it is!" cried Madame Razz.

"It's a *ginger-bread* house!" exclaimed She-Ra.

"It's the home of my old teacher, Madame Whizz," said Madame Razz. "And here she is!" A little old lady with white hair and rosy cheeks came out to meet them as Swift Wind landed lightly on the grass in front of the house.

With cries of delight, the two old friends threw their arms around one another.

"I'll leave you to catch up on all your news," said She-Ra. "Swift Wind and I will take a look at these beautiful mountains." She leapt on to Swift Wind's back. "Have a nice gossip," she cried. "I'll be back in time to take you home." Then Swift Wind rose into the air and went skimming away over the hills.

Once out of sight of the ginger-bread house,
She-Ra set Swift Wind down and left him to graze
while she lay on the soft grass and watched the
white clouds sail across the blue sky.

It was late in the afternoon before She-Ra returned
to the ginger-bread house.

As she and Madame Razz were about to leave,
Madame Whizz handed her old pupil a small parcel.
"I almost forgot," she said. "It's your birthday. Many
happy returns of the day!"

"Everyone else has forgotten it's my birthday," said Madame Razz, sadly. "You are the only person who has remembered." She opened the parcel. Inside was an elegant tea cup and saucer.

"It's magic, of course," said Madame Whizz. "Whenever you feel like a cup of tea it will fill up, just the way you want it. Try it!"

Madame Razz said, "I feel like a cup of tea!" And, immediately, the cup filled up with steaming tea. Madame Razz took a sip. "Just as I like it!" she cried. "Milk and two sugars!"

As Swift Wind rose into the air, Madame Whizz stood outside her ginger-bread house and waved until her visitors were out of sight.

"Ah, well," sighed Madame Razz. "I suppose it was something that *one* person remembered my birthday."

She-Ra smiled quietly to herself as Swift Wind bore them speedily towards Castle Brightmoon and the surprise party.

Meanwhile, in the Great Hall of Castle Brightmoon, the guests were assembling. It was the greatest celebration any of them could remember. They laughed and chatted to each other, while the Royal Musicians played merry airs to pass the time until the festivities would begin.

Outside, the sun was setting. Evening shadows began to spread across the land. But, in Castle Brightmoon, the walls and ceilings glowed with magic light.

Queen Angella checked the guest list again. Not everyone had arrived. There was no sign of Catra. And until Madame Razz arrived, the party couldn't begin.

Glimmer had been looking out of the window at the darkening sky. Then, she gave a cry. "Here she is! Here comes Madame Razz!"

Against the evening stars she had seen something coming swiftly towards the Castle. It was Swift Wind. On his back was She-Ra. And clinging behind the Princess of Power was Madame Razz!

As Swift Wind swept over Whispering Wood, Madame Razz said, "This will do nicely. You can set me down here."

"In a moment," said She-Ra. "I have a little business to attend to. I'd like you to come along with me. That is, if you have no objection."

"Not at all," said Madame Razz.

The Wood was soon left behind, and Castle Brightmoon lay straight ahead. Lights blazed from every window in the Castle, but there was not a sound as Swift Wind came down outside the entrance. The great doors stood wide open.

She-Ra helped Madame Razz to dismount. "Just go straight in," she said. "I'll join you inside in a moment."

Wondering, Madame Razz walked through the entrance, along a wide corridor, and into the Great Hall.

As Madame Razz stepped into the Great Hall, the Royal Trumpeters blew a loud fanfare. This was followed by loud cheering from the guests.

"SURPRISE! SURPRISE!"

"HAPPY BIRTHDAY, MADAME RAZZ!"

Madame Razz didn't know what to say. She just stood, with tears of happiness running down her cheeks. They hadn't forgotten her birthday after all.

Queen Angella took Madame Razz by the hand
and led her to a seat at the table next to her and
Princess Glimmer. And now, the party really got
going.

The guests sat down to a feast of all manner of
Etherian delicacies. While they ate and drank, there
were musicians and jugglers and acrobats to entertain
them. Madame Razz asked if the Queen would
object to her using her own tea cup. And everyone
watched in amazement as the magic cup provided an
endless supply of tea!

Suddenly there was a stir by the door of the Great Hall. Catra had arrived, with Clawdeen by her side.

"Welcome, Catra," called Queen Angella. "And you too, Clawdeen."

"Thank you," said Catra. She looked around her, then at the masses of presents. Among them was the metal cat.

"I see that you received my gift, Madame Razz," she purred.

"Yes, thank you," said Madame Razz. "It's very – er – pretty."

"It is more than pretty," said Catra. "It is very clever. Would you like me to show you what it does?"

"Oh, yes!" cried Madame Razz.

"Yes! Show us what it does!" cried everyone else.

Catra lifted the cat and placed it on a small table in the centre of the Hall. Then, she pressed a secret lever, and stood back as the metal animal began to whirr and buzz!

Nothing else happened for several moments. Then Glimmer cried, "Look at the eyes. The cat's eyes are glowing!"

The dull black eyes were indeed beginning to shine with a weird light. It grew brighter and brighter. But, strangely, the light did not shine out on to the table, the walls, or anything else. Something terrible was happening instead. It was not light, but darkness, coming from the cat's eyes. Two beams of black shadow reached out, darkening the hall in front of it.

Then, the mechanical cat began to move. Slowly it turned its head this way and that. And everywhere it turned its head, the light in the Great Hall of Castle Brightmoon faded and died.

"Stop it!" cried the Queen. "Immediately, Catra! I command you!"

Bow leapt from his seat. But in that moment, the last of the light died. In the pitch darkness Catra laughed.

"You made a great mistake inviting me to Madame Razz's birthday party."

In the darkness, everyone fell over everyone else as they tried to grab Catra and Clawdeen. There was faint starlight coming through the tall windows. But it was not enough to pierce the thick shadow which filled the Great Hall.

Tables were knocked over. Dishes fell with a crash to the floor. And through all the uproar, Catra could be heard calling to Clawdeen, "We who can see in the dark have no need of lights! Now, which of these pretty presents would suit us best? Here is a

fine cloak made from moonbeams and stardust. Or a pair of matching seven-league boots? I rather fancy this...!"

Catra stopped. There came a strange noise. It came from outside the Great Hall, from a distant part of the Castle. It was getting closer and louder every second.

With a clatter, the door from the Castle kitchens burst open, and a blaze of bright light sent Catra's magic shadows fleeing before it.

"It's the Twiggets!" cried Adora, who had changed from She-Ra and slipped in during the feast.

"It's their surprise present for Madame Razz!" cried Bow.

A crowd of Twiggets came marching into the Hall. At the tops of their squeaky little voices they sang:

"HAPPY BIRTHDAY TO YOU!
HAPPY BIRTHDAY TO YOU!
HAPPY BIRTHDAY, MADAME RAZZ!
HAPPY BIRTHDAY TO YOU!"

On their shoulders they bore a giant birthday
cake...ablaze with candles. A thousand and nine
candles, to be precise!

Catra cowered away from the sudden bright light.

Clawdeen turned her eyes from the brightly lit
cake and sprang back. Her tail caught the table that
held the metal cat. With a crash it toppled to the
floor, and the cat shattered into a thousand pieces.
The magic shadows vanished from the Great Hall.

The Twiggets stopped singing. They looked around them at the mess. Furniture was overturned. The floor was covered with spilt food and drink. People were still picking themselves up from where they had fallen in the darkness. And in the middle of everything lay the smashed remains of the evil, green metal cat.

"What happened?" asked the youngest Twigget. "Have we missed a special party game?"

"You arrived just in time," said Kowl, flying down from where he had perched for safety on a roof beam. "That wicked Catra and her furry friend Clawdeen were up to their mischievous tricks again."

"What *I* should like to know," said Madame Razz, "is how did you know how many candles to put on the cake? We ladies tend to be shy about telling our age!"

"If you had been much younger," said Kowl, "there might not have been *enough* candles to spoil Catra's plan."

"Where is Catra?" asked Adora.

"Never mind Catra," said the oldest Twigget. "Let's have some birthday cake."

Queen Angella called for the servants, who began to slice and pass round Madame Razz's birthday cake.

"It's a pity that Catra and Clawdeen couldn't stay," said Madame Razz. "It's not every day that a person has a thousand and ninth birthday. I would have liked to give them each a piece of cake, at least."

Kowl had been perched on a window sill, munching his slice of cake. He looked out.

"There they go!" he cried.

In the moonlight, Catra could be seen making her escape astride Clawdeen. Madame Razz leaned out. "Come back," she called. "You didn't get your cake!"

She paused. "Silly me," she said. "I'll use magic. Madame Whizz showed me this afternoon where I was getting it wrong."

She said the magic words, waved her arms, and the top section of the cake sailed through the window. "Catch!" she cried. But it was too late. The cake hit Catra and Clawdeen in a great splatter of icing, marzipan and other sticky things.

"Oh, well," said Madame Razz. "Cats *do* lick themselves clean, so it won't be wasted. Now, let's get on with my birthday party."